ICE RIVER

BY

PHYLLIS GREEN

DRAWINGS BY

JIM CROWELL

ADDISON-WESLEY

for my father

Young Scott Books by Phyllis Green

The Fastest Quitter In Town
Ice River

 Young Scott Books

Text Copyright © 1975 by Phyllis Green
Illustrations Copyright © 1975 by Jim Crowell
All Rights Reserved
Addison-Wesley Publishing Company, Inc.
Reading, Massachusetts 01867
Printed in the United States of America
First Printing

WZ/WZ   9/75   02582

Library of Congress Cataloging in Publication Data

Green, Phyllis.
  Ice river.

  SUMMARY: An accident on the river brings a young
boy closer to his step-father.

  [1. Family life—Fiction] I. Crowell, Jim,
1936–   illus. II. Title.
PZ7.G82615Ic   [Fic]   74-28382
ISBN 0-201-02582-5

It was hard for Dell Carling to say goodbye
to his dad.
"Why can't I live with you?" he asked.
His father made a fist and pretended to sock Dell's
jaw. "Because, buddy, your mother needs you."
"But she has John Gray now."
"You be nice to your step-father, hear? He likes
you, Dell," his father said. "Now, we'll get
together buddy. Every other Sunday, pal. I'll look
forward to it."

On his father's Sundays, Dell would wait all day. His father didn't show up. In four months he had not shown up once. The first few times he phoned with an excuse. Then he stopped phoning. Dell kept waiting. His mother would say, "Go over and see Izzy. I'll call if your dad comes."

"I'll wait," Dell would say.

His mother would hug him. "I know the feeling," she'd say.

In January his mother and John told him they were going to have a baby. They hoped he would be happy.

He talked to his dog about it. "Oh Mutt, you're all I have now. It's just you and me."

Mutt licked Dell's hands as if he understood.

Dell's best friend was Izzy Rito. In the winter they ice skated every day after school on the pond behind Izzy's house. Mutt always came along and skidded around the ice, chasing the boys and knocking them down.

One day in early March when the boys reached
Dell's house, there was a note on the gate. It said
that his mother and John were at the doctor's and
they might be late for dinner.

"The key is under the mat," it said. "If you need
anything, Mrs. Murdoch is home."

Dell turned to Izzy and closed his eyes. "I am
RAYMONDO, the great KNOW-IT-ALL. I see
all and know all. There will be a note on the front
door that says the same thing."

Izzy looked toward the door. "Hey, there is a piece
of white paper there! Hey, that's great!"

Dell said, "There will also be the same note on the
back door, the kitchen table, the refrigerator, the
television and the toy box."

"Gee, how do you know?" Izzy asked.

Dell opened his eyes. "Because I am RAYMONDO,
the great KNOW-IT-ALL. And because I
know my mother. She always writes me about fifty
notes."

Izzy nodded. "She worries about you."

Mutt came around from the back of the house. Dell kicked the fence. The dog stuck his nose through an opening and Dell petted it.

"Do you want to come skating, boy?" he asked Mutt. The big tail wagged its answer. Dell opened the gate and slapped his leg. "C'mon, Mutt," he called.

He got his skates from the garage and they were
on their way to Izzy's pond.
"How come your mom's going to the doctor so
much?" Izzy asked.
"Something's wrong. She spends lots of time in
bed. I think she cries, too."
When they reached Izzy's house, Dell and Mutt
waited outside while Izzy went to get his skates.
"Don't let your dog bark. I don't want to bother
Mom. Do you smell that? She's been making pasta
all morning and now she's cooking the ravioli."

Izzy was soon back with his skates. He rubbed his
stomach and rolled his eyes.
"I can't wait for dinner. My mom's ravioli is the
greatest."
While the boys put on their skates Mutt went out
on the pond. He started running and sliding across
the ice.
Izzy said, "Two more lessons and Mutt will be the
lead act in the Ice Follies."

Suddenly there was knocking on the window. Dell and Izzy looked up at the house.

Izzy's mother was shouting at them and shaking her finger. Izzy put his head in his hands.

"Oh no, she saw us. That's what I was afraid of."

Mrs. Rito opened the window so they could hear her.

"Izzy, Izzy, Izzy, I told you this morning. No more skating on the pond. It's going to be an early spring. The ice is getting thin."

Izzy nodded to her. She closed the window.

Dell said, "She worries about you."

"Now what do we do?"

"Hey, Iz," Dell said, "We could go to the ice rink in the park."

"Ugh. Girls go there."

"Hey, let's go down to the river. Man it's really thick there. I walked by Saturday and saw some kids playing hockey. C'mon Iz. It's really thick. Honest."

"But the ravioli . . ."

"Your mom will heat it up. Let's just go for a little while."

The ice looked good on the river. They could only
skate near the shore because the ice breakers had
carved out the middle of the river for the boats to
get through.

Mutt was first on the ice. He started to run and went into a slide, his legs out flat on the ice. Izzy gathered up some snow from the shore line and packed it into an ice ball.

"Lookie here, Mutt," he called. "Lookie at the rabbit."

He threw the ice ball. "Go chase the rabbit, Mutt. Go get him."

Mutt ran after the ice ball, sliding and rolling across the ice.

The boys skated after him. When Mutt got to the ice ball he sniffed it. Then he rolled it with his nose. Then he held it in his teeth. Then he ate it.

Izzy bumped against Dell and fell down on the ice laughing. "Oh that dumb dog. He ate the *rabbit*!"

"Wait!" Dell said. "Ladies and gentlemen. Boys and girls. We'll have to cancel the egg hunt this year. My dog, Mutt Carling, has just eaten the Easter Bunny."

Izzy burst into giggles. "Let's see if he'll do it again."

He got some snow and made another ice ball. He threw it far out on the ice, near the middle of the river.

"That's real power," Izzy said as they skated out
to find it.

Mutt beat them. He stood at the edge of the ice
barking.

"He doesn't know what to do," Dell said. "The ice
ball went into the water."

Izzy skated up and made a neat stop at the edge of
the thick ice. "What a dumb day for Peter Rabbit
to go for a swim. Wait till Mr. McGregor finds
out."

"Ha ha, funny man," Dell said. "You're lucky my
dog didn't go in after it. Hey, I think I'm starving.
Let's go home."

Dell turned around. He noticed that something
seemed to be wrong. He felt as if he were moving
even though he was standing still. He blinked his
eyes. He looked at Izzy. By the look on Izzy's face
Dell could tell Izzy felt it too. What was it? He got a
strange feeling. He started to skate to shore. Wait!
They *were* moving. Something *was* wrong. There
was nowhere to skate to!

They were on a great chunk of ice about twenty feet long that had broken off from the mass of ice connected to the shore.

"We're on an ice floe! We can't get back!"

The ice moved with the flow of the river current. The boys helplessly watched the slowly passing shore line. They felt as if they were part of a bad dream. Mutt ran to each edge of the ice. He began to whimper. Dell and Izzy stared at each other. They knew they were in trouble.

"What should we do?" Izzy whispered.

"I think we better scream," Dell said.

They shouted for help. Their voices sounded icy and shallow. Would anyone hear?

"It's getting dark," Dell said. He looked at Izzy and saw him shiver. "A boat will come by."

Izzy shivered again. "Look how fast we're moving," he said.

At last they saw a man on the shore running with
his German Shepherd. They called out to him. The
man yelled back.
"What did he say?" Izzy asked.
"I think he's going to get help," Dell said.

Twenty minutes passed and they were far from
where they had seen the man and the German
Shepherd.
"Maybe he didn't understand," Izzy said. "It's so
dark."

"Look!" Dell shouted, "A boat. It's coming to get us."

"And a helicopter!" Izzy yelled.

The boat was a good distance from them but in a few minutes the helicopter was right over them. The boys waved and yelled.

The wind and the noise of the helicopter scared Mutt. He started jumping and whining and running around in circles.

"It's all right, Mutt," Dell called but his words were lost in the roar of the copter.

Mutt ran and slid. His legs flattened out. He slid right to the edge of the ice floe and down into the black cold water.

"Mutt!" Dell screamed. "Izzy, Mutt's gone! Swim, boy, swim!" he called to the dog.

Dell saw Mutt's head and then he saw it go down into the water again.

At times their ice floe came within five feet of the shore ice. "Let's try to jump," Dell said. "We'll take off our skates. We can make it."

"We can't jump that far. We'll drown," Izzy said. "That water's freezing."

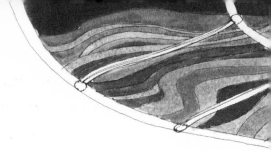

The helicopter lowered the rope ladder for the boys to climb up.

"I'm a good swimmer," Izzy said. He jumped in after Mutt.

In a few seconds he came up and looked at Dell. "I can't find him, Dell."

"Oh Mutt," Dell said. "Oh Mutt, oh . . . Mutt, Mutt."

"Give me a hand," Izzy said. "I'm frozen." Dell reached out to help Izzy on the ice when the edge started cracking. He stepped back toward the middle.

"Help me," Izzy said. "I'm going down." Dell laid flat on the ice. "Grab my hand, Iz." Izzy reached for it. He missed and disappeared into the black water.

The men on the helicopter were shouting at Dell. Izzy, Izzy, he thought, you've *got* to come up. He heard a splash. "Is that you Iz?" he called.

There was no answer and it was too dark now to
see. Suddenly he felt Izzy's cold wet hands touching
his.
"Hang on Izzy!"

He pulled. Then he realized there was a man
holding onto his legs, helping him pull. They both
lay flat on the ice. The man pulled Dell and Dell
pulled Izzy. It seemed to take forever.
Finally the man said, ''O.K. boy, your friend is on
the ice again. That was a close one.''

"But my dog . . ." Dell said.
The boat touched the side of the ice floe. The man
lifted the wet Izzy into a sailor's arms.
"Mutt!" Dell called.
"I'm sorry," the man said. He helped Dell into the
boat.

When they got to the dock a police car drove up
with Mrs. Rito. Izzy was on a stretcher, covered
with blankets, and he was being loaded onto an
ambulance. Mrs. Rito ran to him. She was
screaming and shaking and sobbing.
Dell looked around. Had they radioed his folks?
Where was everyone?

Another police car stopped. John Gray ran out. He threw his arms around Dell and buried him in his chest.

"Thank God," he kept saying.

"Does Mom know Mutt's gone?" Dell asked.

"Your mother doesn't even know about you. She's in the hospital, Dell. She . . . lost the baby."

"Mutt. And the baby?" Dell started to cry.

John hugged him again. "Thank God we didn't
lose you."
The policeman drove them back to the house.
There they got in John's car and drove down the
river highway looking and calling for Mutt.
Dell wasn't sure of the place where Mutt had gone in
the water. They walked around in the cold, calling.
They drove up and down the river highway shouting "Mutt" out the car windows. Finally they had
to give up.
They went to a restaurant for dinner.

When they got back to the house, the phone was ringing. It was Dell's father.

"Heard you had a little excitement. Everything O.K.?" he asked.

"Mutt's gone," Dell said.

"I always liked Mutt," his father said. "How's the Rito boy?"

"He'll be O.K."

His father coughed. "I wanted to rush right over when I heard. If you're sure you're O.K., I'll see you Sunday."

"See you Sunday," Dell said.

He put the phone on the hook. He felt old, older than his father. He saw John looking at him. "That was my dad," he said. "He says he'll come on Sunday. Of course he won't come. But he'll want to. That's what's important."

"Feel like a game of Ping-Pong or would you rather go to bed?" John asked.

"I'm never too tired for Ping-Pong," Dell said.

On the way down to the basement he said, "When you see Mom at the hospital tomorrow, tell her about Mutt. And tell her I'm sorry about the baby. I always wanted a little brother."

The Ping-Pong game was close because Dell was a good player. It ended with John winning 21–19. When Dell went to pick up the ball, he suddenly stepped on it, crunching it flat.

He sat on the bottom step and hid his face in his hands. His body shook. He couldn't stop it. And he couldn't stop the big tears that rolled down his cheeks and dripped from his chin to the basement floor. Finally he sniffed loudly and wiped his nose. "I'm sorry. It's just that I lost everything today."

John picked up the flat Ping-Pong ball. "So that's what it looks like when you step on it? There've been times I've wanted to do that myself."

"Really?" Dell asked.

John took Dell's hand and stood him up. They
walked up the steps arm in arm.
"Do you think we should leave the gate open
tonight just in case Mutt comes home?" Dell
asked.

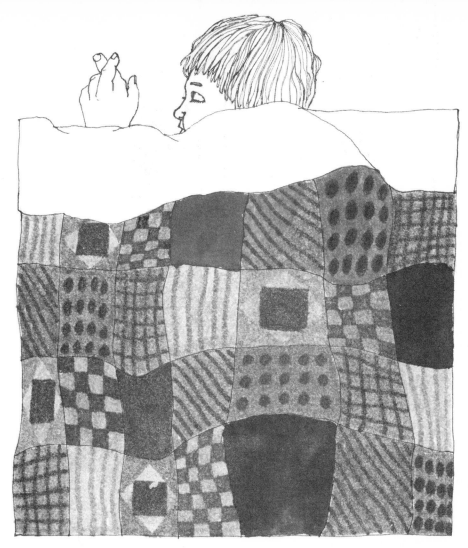

"Oh definitely," John said, "we want to leave the gate open. I'll do that now while you get ready for bed."

Dell was exhausted. He fell into bed. But just before he went to sleep he said a prayer and crossed his fingers.

About two o'clock in the morning there was a
painful cry that touched through the walls of the
house. John Gray sat up in bed. He couldn't tell if
it was the sound of a boy crying in his sleep or the
sound of a dog crying to get in.
He got up to see.

He looked in Dell's room. Dell was curled up in bed, sound asleep. The blankets half covered his face.

Then John heard a small scratching noise at the front door. He ran down the stairs and opened it. Mutt was slumped on the porch, looking up at him.

"Dell!" yelled John. "Your dog's home! Mutt's home!"

John picked up the big wet dog and carried him
into the kitchen.
"Good boy, Mutt. I know somebody that's going
to be glad to see you."
Snow and ice were stuck to Mutt's feet and face
and body. John turned on the oven to warm him.
Dell, half-asleep, ran into the kitchen.

He fell to the floor and started hugging Mutt.
"Mutt, you made it. I knew you'd make it. You just
had to."
"I'll close the front door and get some towels,"
John said.
Dell moved Mutt closer to the oven.
"Do you want some food, boy? Some water?"
John came back in the room carrying two big beach
towels. He smiled.
"Here, Dell," he said. "You dry Mutt and I'll dry
you."
Dell laughed as they both started rubbing Mutt
dry.
"You're pretty wet yourself!"

Finally Mutt stood up and shook his fur.
"Oh no!" John said. "I already took a shower today."
"He feels better," Dell said. "See, he's going to be O.K. Boy, am I lucky."
When Mutt was dry, Dell fed him a little food and gave him some water to drink. John turned off the oven.

"I think it's time for myself, my boy and his dog to hit the sack," he said. "But first young man," he said to Dell, "it's into dry pajamas for you."

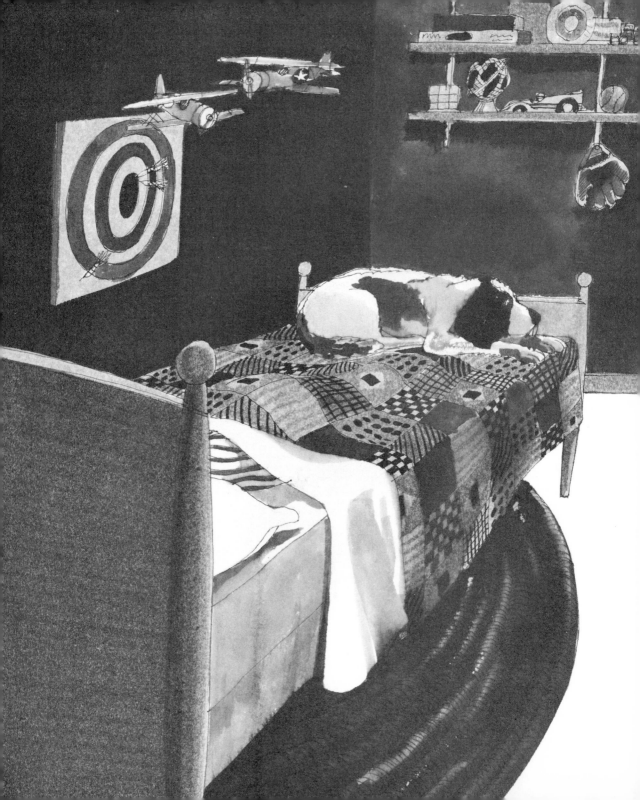

Soon Dell was under the covers and Mutt was
asleep and snoring on top of the covers.
John leaned in the doorway. He saluted Dell.
"What a day," Dell said.
John nodded. "I think we'll remember it. Good-
night, Dell. Pleasant dreams."

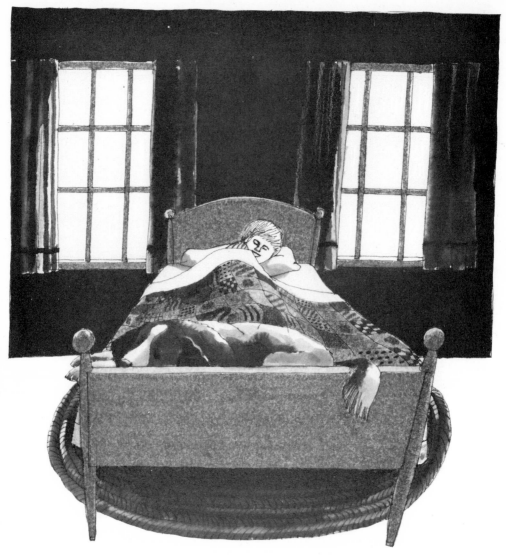

Dell rolled over on his stomach and dug his head
into the pillow. When he heard John start to walk
down the hall, he lifted his head from the pillow
and softly called, "Don't let the bedbugs bite."